Meowth, t

Pokémon

#2

junior

There are more books about Pokémon for younger readers.

Meowth, the Big Mouth

#2 POKÉMON junior

Adapted by Bill Michaels

SCHOLASTIC INC.
New York Toronto London Auckland Sydney
Mexico City New Delhi Hong Kong

ISBN 0-439-15417-0

12 11 10 9 8 7 6 5 4 3 2 1   0 1 2 3 4 5 6/0

Printed in the U.S.A.

First Scholastic printing, April 2000

CHAPTER ONE

You're Invited!

The sun was rising in Pallet Town. It shone on Ash Ketchum's house. Ash was training. He wanted to be the world's greatest Pokémon Master. His friends, Brock and Misty, were helping him. And Pikachu, Ash's first Pokémon, was always by his side.

Ash and Brock were doing their exercises on the porch. Pikachu was working out, too.

"One, two, three, four," said Ash.

"*Pi, pi, pi, pi*," said Pikachu. It was counting just like Ash.

"There is nothing I like better than a good workout," said Ash.

"*Pikachu!*" said Pikachu. *Me, too!*

Inside, Misty

was having a cup of tea with Togepi. Togepi was Misty's little Pokémon. "Those guys are not working hard," she said. "They get more exercise lifting the remote control!"

"*Togi, togi*," said Togepi. *No kidding!*

Mr. Mime was sweeping the driveway of Ash's house. It noticed a mailman on his bike.

"Special delivery!" said the mailman.

Mr. Mime brought the letter to

Ash and his friends. This is what
it said:

> You are invited
> to Hollywood
> to see a new movie.
> It is called
> *Pokémon in Love.*

Ash, Pikachu, Misty, and Brock
all had worked on the movie.
Misty's Pokémon Psyduck was
supposed to be the lead!

"Wow! Hollywood!" said Misty.
"I will see real movie stars!"

Misty and Brock imagined how
great Hollywood would be. They

could not wait to get there!

"You go have fun," said Ash.
"I will just stay here. I will train
for the Pokémon League." Ash
wanted to prove his skills as a
Pokémon trainer.

"Oh, too bad!" said Brock.

"We will miss you," said Misty.

Ash's friends were teasing him.
They really wanted him to come.

Ash thought about it. How could
he miss the chance to see the
stars? "Okay," he said. "I will go!"

"*Pika-pika-pi!*" said Pikachu.
Hooray for Hollywood!

CHAPTER TWO

"We Are Stars!"

Jessie and James had heard about the new movie, too. So they headed out to Hollywood.

Jessie, James, and Meowth formed Team Rocket. Team Rocket was always trying to capture Ash's Pikachu. They collected rare Pokémon, and they

knew how special Pikachu was!
Meowth was pretty special, too.
It was the only talking Pokémon!

The first thing Team Rocket
saw in Hollywood was a big poster
for *Pokémon in Love*.

"James, I cannot wait to go to
the movie opening," said Jessie.

"But I did not get an invitation,"
said James. "Did you?"

"We do not need invitations,"
said Jessie. "We are the stars!"

"But all they have to do is
throw us out," James said.

"You are so silly, James," said

Jessie. "We are going to be famous!"

Jessie and James looked at each other. They were excited!

"Lights!" said James.

"Camera!" said Jessie.

"Action!" they said together.

"Cut!" said Meowth.

Jessie and James were shocked. Why did Meowth want to stop their fun?

"Hollywood is a place I would like to forget," Meowth said. Meowth was thinking about things that happened when it was young, a long, long time ago. . . .

CHAPTER THREE

Meowth Tells Its Tale

Meowth wandered the streets. It thought about the time when it was just a little Meowth.

"When I was little, no one loved me. I was alone. No family, no friends, no home.

"I was hungry all the time. My stomach was always empty,

and so was my heart.

"I was always hunting for scraps of food. But I never found much to eat. One day, I ended up at a summer camp for children. I was so hungry, even a pile of baseballs looked good enough to eat. The baseballs were hard. They tasted like cardboard. They were not even good for me!

"Then a camp counselor saw what I was doing. He was very angry. 'Get away from there!' he shouted. He tied me to a string and hung me from

a tree branch. I could not move!

"I cried myself to sleep. I was so sad! But then something woke me up. It was a bright light!

"The campers were watching a movie outside. It was called *That Darn Meowth.* It was about a family with a pet Meowth. The family loved their Meowth. And their Meowth loved them. They

gave it great food, like ice cream and fried chicken.

"*That is the life!* I thought. I knew that movies were made in Hollywood. So I knew that was where I should go.

"'I am going to Hollywood!' I shouted. I was so excited that I burst free from the branch. 'Hollywood is the place where there is ice cream, and chicken, and a family waiting for me!'"

CHAPTER FOUR

The Bright Lights of Hollywood

Meanwhile, Ash, Misty, and Brock had arrived in Hollywood. They were excited. Pikachu thought it would like to star in a movie. *"Pika-pi! Pika-pi!"* sang Pikachu. *Gotta dance!*

But Hollywood was not what they thought it would be. The

streets were a mess.

"This block looks pretty busted to me," said Misty.

"Now let me see," said Brock. "The map says that the movie theater should be right here."

"This must be the place!" cried Ash. But the movie theater was old and dirty. It looked like no one had been there in years!

Just then, the movie's director jumped out of the building. "That is right, film fans," he said in a loud voice. "This is the place! Get ready to see the hit new movie, *Pokémon in Love*."

"*Pika?*" asked Pikachu. *Should we go in?*

"I guess so," said Ash. "I still want to see ourselves in the movie!"

———

Jessie and James were in Hollywood, too. They were talking to Meowth.

"Meowth, you never told us you had been here before!" said Jessie.

"There are things I like to keep private," said Meowth.

"Like what?" asked James.

Meowth did not want to answer. "You two go ahead," it said. "I have some things I want to take care of."

Jessie and James were confused. But they left Meowth alone.

Meowth was thinking about the first time it came to Hollywood, many years ago. . . .

CHAPTER FIVE

Meowth's Story: Love at First Sight

"I finally arrived in Hollywood. But it was not like I thought it would be. It was not a good place for a Pokémon. There was no ice cream and no fried chicken. They chased me away. I had to steal scraps of food.

"*Nobody cares about me,*

I thought one day. *My life is at a dead end.*

"Just then, I saw two red eyes flashing. Out of the shadows stepped a Persian. It was with a gang of wild Meowth. They looked scary!

"The Persian spoke to me. *'Persian, persian,'* it said. *'You may have some of my food.'*

"I could not believe it. I was starving!

It made me so happy to eat! This Persian could get food for me. So I joined its gang.

"Now I was not hungry anymore. I stayed close to the Persian. But I still did not have a family to love.

"And then one day I met Meowzy. I saw it from across the street. It was love at first sight. Meowzy sat on a pink pillow. It wore a collar with diamonds. It looked like a princess.

"*I have to meet this Pokémon,* I thought. I rushed over to see it.

Screech! I ran so fast that I almost got run over! But I did not care. I would do anything for such a beautiful Meowth. But Meowzy just looked at me and turned up its nose.

"Then Meowzy's owner came to pick it up. The owner drove a fancy car. She kept Meowzy in a diamond Poké Ball.

"'*Meowth, me-meowth,*' Meowzy told me.

'She is a rich lady. She can buy me anything I want. And you? You are not even human. You are just a street Meowth.'

"Meowzy turned its back on me and hopped into the fancy car.

"My heart was breaking. I was not rich enough for Meowzy. Sadly, I watched Meowzy drive away."

CHAPTER SIX

The Story Continues

"I did not want to give up on Meowzy. I wanted to win its love. *I will have to be more than a Pokémon,* I decided. *I will have to learn to walk and talk like a human.*

"I started walking on two legs instead of four. It was hard work.

And it was tough to catch food
that way. I could not run as fast.
I almost got caught stealing!

"I spent every night at the
Hollywood School for Girls.
I watched the girls
in their ballet
class. I listened
to the girls'
spelling
lessons. I tried to
talk clearly, just like
the girls. I spent hours
and hours practicing
and learning.

"'She sells seashells by the seashore,' said the girls.

"'. . . by duh she-shore,' I said slowly.

"At first I was not very good at speaking like humans. Night after night, I practiced. And bit by bit, I got better.

"'She sells seashells by the seashore,' said the girls.

"'She sells seashells by the seashore,' I repeated. *Hey, who knows what it means? I thought. At least I can say it!*

"I got a book that showed the

alphabet. Slowly, I learned how to read.

"*R is for rocket.*

"That was the first word I learned. (And maybe that is why I like Team Rocket so much!)

"*H is for happy.*

"*M is for marriage.*

M is for Meowzy, too, I thought. *We could be so happy together.*

"I practiced and practiced. Finally, I was ready to meet Meowzy again."

CHAPTER SEVEN

Meowth and Its Mouth

"The next day, I went to find Meowzy. I walked up to it on two legs. 'Meowzy!' I called. I said its name — just like a human. 'Look at me now!'

"'*Meowth?*' said Meowzy lazily.

"'See, I can stand on two legs just like a human does,' I said.

'And I can talk human talk, too!'

"Meowzy yawned.

"'I am just like a human now.
And I brought you some flowers!'

"Meowzy shook its head.

"*Meowth. Me-me-meowth
meowth,*" Meowzy said. *You are
not a human and you are not a*

*Pokémon. You are worse than
before. Now you are a freak!*

"'Noooooo!' I cried. Its words
scratched my heart like a claw.

"'Meowzy thinks I'm a freak?' I
shouted. "'Well, I will show it. I
will become the richest, most
powerful freak ever. One day
Meowzy will beg for my love!'

"But Meowzy never did. So I
joined Team Rocket. I hoped it
would make me rich and powerful. I have had many adventures.
But I do not know if Meowzy
would still think I am a freak."

CHAPTER EIGHT

The Old Gang Returns

Now Meowth was older and
wiser. It was back in Hollywood
with Jessie and James.

"I guess Meowzy does not live
here anymore," said Meowth
sadly.

But just then, Meowth saw one
of the old Persian gang.

"Hiya . . . bud," said Meowth.

The wild Meowth stepped back. Behind it, Meowth saw the old gang leader, Persian.

"*Per? Persian, per?*" said the Persian to Meowth. *Is it you? You look almost human.*

"I bet you want me to join the gang again," said Meowth. "Well, I can walk like a human. And I can talk like a human. So it would be good to have me in your gang."

"*Perrr,*" said the Persian. *Oh, yes.*

"Well, I am sorry to disappoint

you, pal. But I am sticking with Team Rocket."

"*Persian, per!*" said Persian. *You must come back!*

"My mind is made up," said Meowth. "And nothing is going to change it."

"*Persian!*" said Persian sharply. All of a sudden, from behind Persian, a familiar Pokémon stepped forward.

Meowth could not believe its eyes. It was Meowzy!

"No! Meowzy! What are you doing here?" Meowth cried.

"*Meowth, meowth,*" said Meowzy. *I'm with Persian now.* It hung its head.

"What happened?" asked Meowth.

Meowzy told Meowth all about its life. A few years ago, its owner ran out of money. She let Meowzy go on the mean streets. Meowzy had nothing to eat.

"*Me-meowth,*" Meowzy said. *Then Persian took care of me.*

"But you cannot stay with Persian and those bums," said Meowth. "I am here now!"

"*Meow,*" said Meowzy. *Do not ask me to choose!*

"I am getting you out of here right now," said Meowth.

Suddenly, the gang of wild Pokémon surrounded Meowth.

They did not want it to take
Meowzy. Meowth tried to block
them. But it could not reach
Meowzy. It could not get away.

"Help!" cried Meowth.

Then . . .

"Prepare for trouble!"

"Make it double!"

It was Team Rocket!

"Hey, guys," said Meowth.
"Did you really come here to
rescue me?"

"We may be mean and nasty,"
said Jessie. "But we never turn
our backs on a teammate in

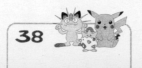

trouble! We saw you with this scruffy gang. So we followed you."

"We cannot let anything bad happen to our little buddy!" said James.

"It is so nice to have real friends," said Meowth. It smiled at Jessie and James.

"We will take care of this gang," said Jessie. "Go Arbok!"

Jessie's Poison Pokémon, Arbok, flew through the air. *"Arbok!"* it cried.

"Weezing, go!" cried James.

Out flew Weezing.

Soon, the air was filled with poison gas. The wild Meowth could not fight Team Rocket! But Persian was not ready to give up Meowzy.

Meowth and Persian sprang at each other. They missed. But Persian hurt itself when it landed. Meowth was ready to pounce. Then Meowzy cried out, *"Meow!"* *No!*

"Meowzy, I am okay!" shouted Meowth.

But Meowzy was not worried about Meowth. It ran past Meowth, straight to Persian. It licked Persian's wounds gently.

"After what Meowth did for it . . ." said Jessie.

". . . it is sticking with Persian?" finished James.

"*Meow, meow. Meowth-meow,*" said Meowzy. *The Persian fed me when I was down and out. It would not be right for me to leave it.*

Meowth was touched. Its eyes filled with tears.

"*Meowth,*" added Meowzy. *And anyway, you are a freak!*

"It called me a freak!" Meowth screamed.

"Maybe you are," said Jessie.

"But you are *our* freak," said James, putting his arm around Meowth.

Meowth smiled. It was good to have what it had always wanted: a family.

CHAPTER NINE

The Show Must Go On

Back at the movie theater, the director showed Ash and his friends the movie.

"Well, what do you think?" he asked when the movie was over. "I have made a new masterpiece, right?"

"I don't know about master-

pieces," said Ash. "But I did not see *us* in the whole movie!"

"Neither did I!" added Misty.

"My film is about Pokémon," said the director. "So I cut you out!" He faked a tear. "It hurt me to do it," he said.

"It hurt us even more!" said Ash.

"Then why did you ask us to come?" asked Misty.

"Because I could not get any real stars," said the director.

Just then, they all heard a familiar voice.

"If you wanted stars . . ."

"You should have invited us!"

It was Jessie and James and Meowth.

"Team Rocket blast off at the speed of light!" said Jessie.

"Surrender now or prepare to fight!" said James. "But you will have to talk to my agent," he added.

"That is showbiz," said Meowth.

"What do you want this time?" asked Ash.

"Oh, nothing," said Jessie. "We just want to put on a show!"

Jessie, James, and Meowth did

a tap dance.

"It looks
like Team
Rocket is
dancing off
again!" said
Jessie. And they disappeared with
a *ping*.

"I guess our movie career is
over," said Brock.

"Before it even started," said
Misty.

"*Togi!*" said Togepi. *No fair!*

"*Pika pika chu chu,*" said Pikachu. *So long, Hollywood.*

"Who cares!" said Ash. "I am getting out of this crazy town. I am going back to Pallet Town to train for the Pokémon League." He looked at his friends. "Want to come?"

"Sure do!" said Misty.

"You bet," said Brock.

They started on their way.

Pikachu jumped up on Ash's shoulder. "*Pika!*" said Pikachu. *There is no place like home.*

Pikachu to the rescue!

POKÉMON junior™

Chapter Book #3:
Save Our Squirtle!

It's no secret that the evil Team Rocket is out to get Pikachu. But when they kidnap Squirtle to get to the little lightning mouse, they've gone too far! Can Pikachu and pals save their friend in time? Or will the tiny turtle become Team Rocket's newest member?

Catch it in May!